Horseshoes
#2
Jumping
LESSONS

Jumping
LESSONS

Written by Patricia Leitch

HarperTrophy
A Division of HarperCollinsPublishers

This series is for Meg

First published in Great Britain by Lions, an imprint of HarperCollins
Publishers, in 1992.

Jumping Lessons
Copyright © 1992 by Patricia Leitch

For information address HarperCollins Children's Books,
a division of HarperCollins Publishers,
10 East 53rd Street, New York, NY 10022.

Library of Congress Cataloging-in-Publication Data
Leitch, Patricia
Jumping lessons / written by Patricia Leitch.
p.   cm. — (Horseshoes ; #2)
Summary: Although she nearly despairs of ever being able to jump, ten-
year-old Sally wants to participate in a Scottish pageant along with a world-
famous show jumper.
ISBN 0-06-027288-0 (lib. bdg.) — ISBN 0-06-440635-0 (pbk.)
[1. Horse shows—Fiction.   2. Horses—Fiction.   3. Pageants—Fiction.
4. Scotland—Fiction.]   I. Title.   II. Series: Leitch, Patricia.   Horseshoes ; #2.
PZ7.L5372Ju   1996   95-26351
[Fic]—dc20   CIP
                                                                             AC

Typography by Darcy Soper
2   3   4   5   6   7   8   9   10
❖
First Edition

Also by Patricia Leitch

Horseshoes #1
THE PERFECT HORSE

Horseshoes

#2

Jumping

LESSONS

Chapter One

Sally Lorimer stood beside Willow, her dapple-gray horse, scowling. She was watching Thalia ("rhymes with dahlia, which is a flower") Nesbit mounting Tarquin, her finely bred roan. Sally was ten—medium height: not small, not tall; medium size: not fat, not skinny; with thick, shoulder-length brown hair, wide-set blue eyes, and a quirky mouth that turned up at the corners.

"Now watch what I do," Thalia said as she turned Tarquin and rode him toward the first jump.

"What does she think I've been doing?" Sally muttered to Willow. "All week I've been doing nothing but watching her. I can see what she does but I can't do it."

Tarquin stormed up to the jump, his ears sharp, his eyes glinting. He rose over the stacked wooden boxes in a high soaring arc, leaping as if it were a six-foot barricade. He cleared the four other rickety jumps in the same way.

"There," said Thalia. "It's simple. You've got to go with your horse. Bend forward just when he's going to jump. Did you see how I did it?"

Sally had seen only the flying speed of Tarquin, and Thalia riding as she always did, with total confidence. No matter what Tarquin did, Thalia sat there effortlessly, her ancient hard hat crammed on her sunburst of fair hair, her long, lean body at one with her horse.

"Go on," said Thalia. "Give it another shot. And lean forward when Willow jumps."

Sally patted Willow's neck, remounted reluctantly, and trotted Willow in a circle before she cantered toward the first jump. Willow took off accurately, popped over the jump, and cantered gently on with Sally flopped over her neck.

Sally just could not understand what went wrong. Every time Willow jumped, she was thrown down onto Willow's neck when she landed. For five days Thalia had been trying to teach Sally to jump, and there had been absolutely no improvement.

"Go on! Go on!" yelled Thalia. "Don't stop!"

Willow jumped the second jump, and only a desperate grab at a fistful of mane kept Sally from falling off. At the third jump Sally didn't manage to bend forward at all. She was shot out of the saddle at the takeoff and thumped back into it on the other side. Her sudden weight made Willow's hind legs crash into the jump, knocking it down.

As Willow landed from the fourth jump, Sally, left behind again, slid over her shoulder and landed on the ground.

"You don't bend your waist," Thalia said, almost shouting as Sally scrambled back to her feet. "You're always left behind. I keep telling you what to do, but you won't do it. I don't know why Willow keeps on jumping for you."

"You're supposed to be teaching me," Sally shouted back. "I'm trying to do what you tell me, but I can't."

Tears of frustration welled up in her eyes. She wiped them away furiously on her sleeve. "I am *trying* to do what you tell me."

"Then your trying's not worth much."

"Neither is your teaching."

The two girls stood glaring at each other.

"Hot pancakes in the kitchen in half an hour," called Sally's mother from the field gate.

Mrs. Lorimer had been taking Meg and Misty, the Lorimers' two Bearded collies, for a walk on the beach. Coming back, she had seen Sally falling off and heard the two girls shouting at each other.

"And lemonade," she added, calling the Beardies and walking on to Kestrel Manor.

Only three months before, the Lorimer family had lived in a brick house in Matwood, a suburb of Tarent in the northwest of Scotland.

From the first minute they had discovered Kestrel Manor—empty and desolate and for sale—all the Lorimer family had longed to live there. But it had been far, far too expensive. Then Mr. Lorimer's great-uncle Nathan—who had owned a sheep farm in Australia—died, leaving Mr. Lorimer a considerable amount of money. And before long Sally's dream of living at Kestrel Manor and having her own horse had come true.

Kestrel Manor was a stone house with a high tower, battlements, and a courtyard guarded by two enormous stone dogs. It was built on a penin-sula—almost an island—joined to the mainland only by a long driveway lined on each side with copper beech trees. It stood surrounded by over-grown lawns, a kitchen garden buried under weeds, a ruined greenhouse, and a summerhouse perched on the cliff's edge high above the sea.

There was a stable yard with a feed house and tack room and three stalls. The field where Thalia and Sally were riding had been refenced. It was now almost perfect, with a stream and a huge spreading chestnut tree for shelter.

For a minute longer the two girls stood not speaking. Then they both spoke at once.

"Do you want another jump?" Thalia asked.

"If there's pancakes, I suppose we'd better go in."

They stopped, giggled, and the moment was past, almost forgotten as they led their horses to the stable yard and into the cool stalls to take off their tack.

Thalia Nesbit was the same age as Sally. Her parents were divorced, and she lived with her narg—"gran" spelled backward. She kept Tarquin at Kestrel Manor, sharing the stabling and field with Sally and Willow.

"Water! Water!" cried Thalia, setting down a full bucket into Willow's box. "I'm going to give Tarquin a feed. Not much. Just a taste."

"And Willow," Sally said. She looked critically at her horse as Willow buried her muzzle in the water, drinking deeply.

Sally had saved Willow from being sold for

slaughter. She had been skin and bones then, but her weeks of grazing had rounded her out, giving her coat a healthy sheen and her dark eyes a bright sparkle.

Leaning over the half door, Sally watched Willow feeding. She ate delicately, chasing the very last grain of oats around her trough before she turned her attention to the pony nuts.

Sally's heart overflowed with love. Her very own horse. Willow.

"Come on," said Thalia, "or your family will have finished the pancakes." Sally turned and followed Thalia out of the yard, across the grass, and into the house.

She wondered if her mother had seen her falling off. She just didn't know what she was doing wrong—didn't know why she couldn't jump like Thalia. Perhaps she could only ride, not jump. . . .

"Oh no, Sally Lorimer. You're not going to get caught like that again," she told herself severely. "You want to jump and you are going to jump. So there!"

Chapter Two

All the Lorimers were sitting around or on the kitchen table. The air was filled with the mouthwatering smell of newly made pancakes.

"Here they are," said Ben as Sally and Thalia came in. Ben was fifteen, wore glasses, and had thick black hair like his father's. "About time, too," he went on. "We all had to wait for you."

"And we're all drooling," added Mr. Lorimer.

Jamie, who was four and the youngest Lorimer, brought a tray of pancakes across to the table.

"Watch the dogs!" screamed Mrs. Lorimer as Misty jumped up at the pancakes.

Thalia dived and caught the tray, lifting it high above Misty's gray-and-white head.

"You would have had fun with that, you fat greedy old pooch," teased Mr. Lorimer. He ruffled Misty's long hair over her face, making her bark and leap like a Chinese dragon, her back paws solid, her front paws bouncing up and down, from side to side. Meg, who was an elderly black-and-white Beardie, sat down stiffly by Mr. Lorimer's side, fixed him with her unyielding gaze, and began to whine gently.

"The noise!" exclaimed Ben.

Mrs. Lorimer brought butter, and jam made from Kestrel Manor's gooseberries.

They ate—Ben hidden behind the local newspaper; Jamie on the floor; Mr. Lorimer feeding the dogs bits; Mrs. Lorimer telling him not to; Thalia stuffing herself; and Sally, having caught her mother's eye and knowing that she had seen her falling off, nibbling around the edge of her pancake, wondering what would be said.

When they had finished cleaning up, Thalia said thank you and that they'd better be getting back to the horses. Sally began a stealthy retreat to the back door.

"How's the jumping going?" asked Mr. Lorimer, freezing Sally in her tracks.

"Okay," said Thalia.

"Didn't look very okay to me," said Mrs. Lorimer. "From what I've seen, you're either galloping wildly around on Tarquin or Sally is falling off."

"Tarquin jumps best when he's going fast," said Thalia.

"And Willow? Does she jump best when Sally is falling off?"

"Oh, it's not Willow's fault," Sally exclaimed, then clapped her hand over her mouth. She hadn't meant to admit to her parents that anything was wrong.

"Come and sit down for a moment," said Mr. Lorimer. Reluctantly Sally and Thalia came back to the table.

"Tell us, or we can't help you," said Mrs. Lorimer.

"Well, I keep explaining to Sally what to do, but she won't."

"I'm trying," said Sally. "Thalia says I get left behind. Willow jumps absolutely perfectly, and then I just sort of collapse on her neck when she lands."

"She won't bend her waist."

"I do. I do bend my waist, but it never goes right." To her dismay Sally felt tears pricking behind her eyes.

"I think," said her mother comfortingly, "that you need some help."

"How about jumping lessons?" suggested Mr. Lorimer.

"There's nowhere. Absolutely nowhere near here," declared Thalia.

"What about Mr. Frazer's stables? Surely they give riding lessons?"

"But they cost the earth," said Thalia, looking at Mr. Lorimer as if he had suddenly gone completely crazy.

Sally felt her stomach turn to lead and her heart batter against her ribs. She could not possibly, would not ever, go near Mr. Frazer's stables again.

When she had been looking for a horse, they had gone to Mr. Frazer's yard. Sally had ridden Bilbo, a sturdy bay gelding with a clipped mane. When the ride had gone down to the beach, she had been afraid Bilbo would run away with her. She had tried to dismount, fallen off, and refused to get on again. It all seemed a very long time ago and Sally had left the fear of galloping far behind her. She had almost forgotten that she had ever been afraid. But her father's words brought it all back—the blaze of the sun on the wet sand, the plunging hooves of the other horses on the ride, and the shocked, mocking faces when she absolutely refused to get back on Bilbo. Never could she go back to Mr. Frazer's.

"I think I could afford it, thanks to Great-uncle Nathan," said Mr. Lorimer. "No matter what he charges, it will be better than a daughter in the hospital. How often have you fallen off while you've been trying to jump?"

Sally stared blankly in front of her. She honestly didn't know. She had lost count.

"A few times," said Thalia vaguely.

"Lessons," stated Mr. Lorimer. "Most definitely lessons."

"He's got the most super paddock, and an indoor school," said Thalia, eaten up with instant jealousy.

"I'm not going. They'd only laugh at me."

"Lessons for you both," said Mr. Lorimer.

Thalia made a fish-out-of-water noise. "Me too?" she demanded. "I would totally, absolutely love to go. I never, ever imagined that I would have riding lessons at Mr. Frazer's. But you can't mean it? Not really?"

Sally sat frozen. Thalia's enthusiasm washed over her in a wave of icy despair.

"Of course I mean it. No fun for Sally going by herself."

"Hey," said Ben from behind his paper. "Listen to this. 'Torbracken Open House. Lady Muriel Spencer is opening Torbracken House to the public on Saturday the sixteenth of August. There will be demonstrations of Scottish crafts, Scottish country dancing, archery, working sheepdogs, and many more attractions.

"'In the afternoon the Tarentshire Battlers will enact the legend of the wicked steward who tried to steal the estates and lands of Torbracken from his absent master. Extras are required for this pageant, including foot soldiers, mounted followers, and crowd. For further details phone Lady Muriel Spencer at Tarent six-five-four-nine.'"

"We saw them before," said Mrs. Lorimer. "The Battlers. At the Abbey Festival."

"Slashing and stabbing and brandishing," remembered Ben. "They were great."

"Mounted followers?" demanded Thalia. "Do you think they'd want children? Be super if we could be in it."

"Good fun for us all," said Mrs. Lorimer.

Sally said nothing. She had seen her father go quietly from the kitchen and she knew what he was doing. He was phoning Mr. Frazer, inquiring about jumping lessons. Half of Sally wanted to run after her father and stop him, for she could not bear the thought of going back to the stables and seeing Martine Dawes, the riding instructor, again. Not after making such an idiot of herself.

But half of her wanted more than anything to be able to jump like Thalia, wanted to jump with Thalia in the pairs cross-country competition at the Tarent Horse Show. And Sally knew that the only way she could do this was to go to Mr. Frazer's and find out what she was doing wrong.

"They had two muskets. *Kerumph! Kerumpha!*" shouted Ben, charging around the kitchen as he tried to explain to Thalia what the Tarentshire Battlers had been like.

"About ten horses and rows of soldiers with pikes at the ready. And in the end they were all dead," said Ben. He crashed to the floor and was instantly submerged in Beardies.

"You two could come and be dogs of war," he told them as he struggled back to his feet.

All this time Sally was sitting perfectly still, her ears straining to hear her father's footsteps coming back to the kitchen.

"Wasn't there a charge at the end?" said Mrs. Lorimer.

"Flat-out galloping?" cried Thalia, her eyes shining.

"Flat-out galloping charge," Ben told her, grinning at the thought.

"Will there be a battle this time?" asked Mrs. Lorimer.

"If it's the Battlers, there is bound to be a battle," said Ben. "We *must* be in it."

"It's all fixed up," said Mr. Lorimer, coming back. "A course of jumping lessons for you both on your own horses, starting tomorrow morning."

"Aren't you star-dazzled with delight?" demanded Thalia as they turned their horses out.

"No," said Sally. "I'm moon-sick at the thought of meeting Martine Dawes again. And so would you, if you were me."

Before going to sleep, Sally sat at her bedroom window at the top of the tower, looking out over the far reaches of the sea. Standing on one of the windowsills was a tiny crystal unicorn that she had found before they came to live at Kestrel Manor. It was about two inches high with a golden horn, a golden tassel tail, and tiny jeweled eyes that shone dark green and ruby scarlet. Sally had found it lying at the tide's edge. When she put her hand down to pick it up, a wave had carried it to her, leaving it in the palm of her hand.

Sally took it down from the window and stood it in the palm of her hand. In some strange way she was sure it was magic, sure it was the unicorn that had brought them to Kestrel Manor and let her find Willow.

Her new riding things were hanging on the outside of her wardrobe. Very carefully she slipped the unicorn into her jacket pocket.

"Please," she said aloud. "Please don't let me fall off too often. And don't let Martine laugh at me."

Chapter Three

Willow and Tarquin—tack polished, well groomed, with manes and tails brushed out into silken falls of hair—trotted along the road to Mr. Frazer's stables.

"Be quicker if we rode over the beach," Thalia had said. "But we don't want to arrive all covered with seaweed and sand."

Both girls were neatly turned out. Sally was in her new hacking jacket, cream jodhpurs, brown jodhpur boots, and crash cap. Thalia was wearing a black jacket, white jodhpurs, and black boots with her faded green-black hat pressed down on her fizzing fair hair.

The sky was a dazzling azure blue.

"I think," said Thalia, "your dad just might be a saint."

Sally, her stomach leaden, her mouth bone-dry, didn't feel she could totally agree.

"Better walk a bit," suggested Thalia. "Or they'll be sweating before we get there."

Slowed to a walk, the horses looked around

with a bright curiosity. They knew they were going somewhere special.

"What shall I say to Martine?" asked Sally desperately as the stables came into sight.

"Smile," advised Thalia.

Sally tried, but her lips kept settling back into a tight nervous line.

When they turned down the lane to the stables, a black mare and her rubber-legged foal came cantering over to them and followed them along the paddock fence. Tarquin's head shot up and, whinnying with sharp puffs of sound, he pranced along beside the mare and foal. Willow, too, danced excitedly behind Tarquin, clearly saying that never in all her life had she seen anything so extraordinary as the foal.

As they rode into the stable yard, Sally was too busy trying to calm Willow to worry about what Martine would say to her.

Martine was waiting for them at an open stall door. She was wearing a red-and-white checked shirt and navy breeches. Her black hair was cut short and her skin tanned after a summer spent working out-of-doors.

"Has Betsy been showing off her foal?" she asked, coming toward them.

"I think Tarquin wanted to kidnap it," said Thalia.

"All the horses are demented by it," agreed Martine, laughing at Tarquin who was still bouncing up and down like a rocking horse.

"Now, I've met Sally," Martine went on. "Glad to see you're riding again. We all have times when everything goes wrong and I guess our ride together was one of those times. So this is your new horse. She is very nice indeed."

Sally beamed.

"And this is?"

"Thalia Nesbit," said Thalia. "And Tarquin."

"Bit of a firecracker?" asked Martine, patting Tarquin's shoulder.

"He's fast," said Thalia. "But that's how I like him."

"And he looks as if he'd have a jump in him?"

"He'll jump anything," agreed Thalia.

Martine led the way around the side of a row of stalls and held open the gate of a large paddock. At the far end were jumps; the near half was a schooling area.

"Before we start jumping, we'll do some schooling," said Martine. "You can see letters marking out the track. Ride around at a free walk. Tarquin first and Willow about three horse lengths behind."

Sally checked Willow until she was far enough behind Tarquin and then let her walk on.

"Sally, relax your hands," said Martine. "Feel the movement of Willow's head through your fingers. If you hold your hands tight and still at the walk, you'll catch her mouth at every stride. Relax your elbows. Good. Nice contact, Thalia."

Sally concentrated on her riding, becoming aware of Willow's stride and head carriage, and of her seat and hands speaking to her horse. They worked hard, changing from walk to halt, from halt to walk, over and over again.

"Until," said Martine, "you only need to think 'halt' or 'walk' and your horse obeys."

She showed Sally how to sit straight, looking in front of her and not down at her hands, feeling the collar of her jacket against the back of her neck.

"If you look down, you round your back. All your weight goes on your horse's forehand and you've lost the balance we're aiming for."

"Your aids are too sudden," she told Thalia. "You asked Tarquin for a walk, and although he knows you so well, he still thinks you might be asking him to spring into a flat-out gallop. Gently, easily, and sweetly."

Thalia opened her mouth to say she'd always ridden like this but managed to stop herself in time.

They rode at a sitting trot, first with stirrups and then without.

"Best thing in the world for your seat," Martine said, smiling at Sally's expression as she bumped around.

Riding without stirrups didn't seem to make much difference to Thalia, but Sally bumped and joggled and held on to the front of her saddle. She was so busy trying to stay on top of Willow that she hardly noticed three girls who were leaning on the paddock rail watching them.

At last Martine relented. "Prepare to walk. Walk. Take your stirrups back."

Gratefully Sally uncrossed her stirrups and, feeling for them with the tips of her toes, was back to normal.

"Practice without stirrups at home," Martine told them. "Remember, sink down in your saddle. Relax. No pinching with your knees. Now, ride around at a free walk. Sally, look up.

Then we'll go down to the jumps and you can let me see you jumping."

Now that she was quietly walking around, Sally had time to look at the three girls who had been watching them. She was sure she knew one of them—a girl a bit older than herself with styled brown hair, pimply skin, and a stupid giggle that seemed to get louder each time Sally rode past. Her friends both had wavy reddish hair, freckles, and pale blue eyes. They looked like sisters, and their giggling was even louder than the pimply girl's.

As Martine led the way down to the jumps, Sally shivered with a sudden attack of nerves. "This is where you fall off," she thought. "Where you make a fool of Willow." She laid her hand on Willow's shoulder and flicked a strand of mane over to the correct side of her neck. Somehow it made it worse that she was always falling off when her horse jumped so willingly.

"Who are the gigglers?" Thalia asked, reining Tarquin in, waiting for Sally to catch up.

"Don't know," said Sally. She was thinking about jumping, wondering whether it would be better to hold on to a handful of Willow's mane as they cantered up to the jump and then flop down onto Willow's neck as they landed, or to sit back and be thrown out of the saddle as Willow took off.

"Well, the pimply one knows you. That's what they're giggling about, the toads!"

The three girls were following them down to the jumps. Sally twisted around and looked at them intently. At first she couldn't think who they were. Then, with a sinking heart, she recognized the pimply girl. She was the girl who had been riding on a piebald horse the day Sally had fallen off Bilbo and refused to get on again. So that was what they were giggling about.

Martine finished setting up the jumps and came over to Thalia and Sally. She looked sharply at the three girls, but they paid no attention to her.

"Now," she said to Thalia. "Canter around once and then jump those four just as if you were jumping at home."

Thalia nodded, her face beaming. She touched Tarquin into a canter, and the roan sprang forward, his ears pricked and his head high, knowing he was going to jump.

He stormed up to the first jump, clearing it

with miles to spare, while Thalia sat tight and close, urging him on. She cleared all four jumps at the same breakneck speed, and then it was Sally's turn.

Sally began to trot Willow around the paddock, aware of the girls' giggling, of Martine's watching her intently, and of Thalia's standing beside Tarquin, praising him.

"Let her canter on," called Martine, and Sally unwillingly eased her reins a fraction, allowing Willow to canter unevenly up to the first jump. Sally sat back, bumping down on the saddle as Willow jumped.

"Go with your horse," Martine instructed. "Bend your waist."

"Sounds just like Thalia," Sally thought. She leaned forward to grab Willow's mane, collapsing over her neck as they cleared the second jump.

Before Sally found her balance again, Willow had turned and trotted on to the third jump. As she jumped—neatly, willingly—Sally slid over her shoulder. The ground came rushing up to meet her as she fell.

"This is the best part," giggled the pimply girl. "She won't get on again, you'll see."

"Shut up," said Thalia, turning on them. "Just shut up."

Sally scrambled to her feet, still holding on to the reins, and had remounted almost before Martine reached her.

"And that's what happens all the time," said Sally hopelessly.

"It won't happen again, I promise you." Seeing that Sally was all right, Martine marched over to the three girls.

"Off you go, away from here," she told them. "Charlotte, if your tack is still in the disgusting state it was in yesterday, you are not coming on any ride with me. Now off with you. Any more of your nonsense and I'll speak to Mr. Frazer about you.

"We haven't time to do much more today," Martine said, turning back to Sally and Thalia. "Your horses have worked hard and you've done well yourselves. Thalia, you've got to steady Tarquin. Half halts to get his attention. Bring him back onto his quarters and balance him. Small circles at a sitting trot. Changes from walk to trot, trot to walk, and halts. Lighten your aids. I'm sure he'd respond to a whisper if you give him the chance."

Thalia listened carefully, nodding her head and biting her tongue to keep herself from arguing.

"Sally, it's you, not your horse. We need to work on giving you a firm, balanced seat, so lots of exercises when you're on Willow—toe touching, twisting with your arms outstretched, and swinging your legs all the way around—front, side, back, side, and around to the front again. And lots of work at the sitting trot without your stirrups."

"I'll try," said Sally. "Will that really teach me to jump?"

"I promise," said Martine. "Now, when is your next lesson?"

"Not tomorrow but the next day," said Sally.

"Good," said Martine. "We'll concentrate on riding over poles and a small jump."

"Martine! Phone!" a boy called, shouting from the back of the stalls.

"Walk them around a bit and then come up to the yard," Martine said, and ran long-legged toward the stables. As soon as she was out of sight, Charlotte and her two friends reappeared.

"What do they want?" Thalia asked suspiciously as she and Sally rode around the edge of the jumping paddock.

"Hi," called the pimply Charlotte. "We want to ask you something."

"Ig-nore, ig-nore," commanded Thalia in a robotic tone.

"Listen. We want to know why you were jumping such pitiful, tiny jumps?"

"Were you afraid?" echoed one of her friends.

"Don't listen to them," Sally warned, but Thalia had already swung Tarquin around.

"What did you say?" she demanded.

"Are you afraid to jump a real jump?" Charlotte giggled.

"Watch," spat Thalia. "Just stand there and watch me."

The four small jumps Martine had put up were in the middle of the paddock. Around the edge were three jumps about two feet high and one that looked over three feet.

Thalia gathered Tarquin together.

"We'll show them," she whispered. Tarquin sensed her excitement and pranced on the spot, tight as a coiled spring.

They soared over the first three jumps, as Sally had known they would. She turned to tell Charlotte and the others to mind their own business in the future, then realized that Thalia had not finished jumping.

"Don't!" Sally screamed. "It's too high! Stop!" Her voice was a high-pitched shriek.

She heard Charlotte gasp and one of the other girls shout something about Martine, as Thalia rode at the spread of poles.

It seemed to Sally that Thalia was jumping in slow motion. Tarquin rose at the red-and-white poles, climbing on air, like a salmon fighting its way upstream, before he stretched out in a fluid arc and landed far beyond the jump. Throughout all the jumping Thalia had hardly moved in the saddle. Only her hands, light and sensitive, had followed Tarquin's reaching head.

Thalia rode straight up to Charlotte.

"See?" she said. Then she turned Tarquin to ride up to the paddock gate.

"I never knew you could jump like that!" said Sally, trotting Willow to keep up with Tarquin's long stride.

"Well, he is more or less Thoroughbred," said Thalia, trying to sound as if it had been nothing, as if she jumped that height every day. But her lips curled up at the corners with pride in her horse.

As they reached the stables, they both saw Martine at the same time. She was standing waiting for them, her face coldly furious.

"I did not see what I have just seen. If I had seen it, you would go home and never ride here again. Of all the foolish, stupid things to do! While you are on our grounds, Mr. Frazer is responsible for your safety. I left you alone because I thought you had some sense, but obviously I was wrong."

"It was Charlotte," interrupted Sally.

"I do not want to hear any excuses. What would have happened if Tarquin had broken a leg?" she asked, looking directly at Thalia. "Now dismount and lead your horses up to the yard. Wait there while I fetch a brochure for Mr. Lorimer."

Sally and Thalia waited in the yard, not looking at each other. Thalia bit hard on her quivering lower lip.

A car drove into the yard, and Thalia and Sally moved toward the tack room to get out of the way. A notice was pinned to the tack-room wall—a notice about the pageant at Torbracken House. Any child or adult who wanted to take part in the pageant as a mounted follower was to come to a meeting in the indoor school the next morning, when Lady Muriel Spencer would speak to them herself.

"Let's go," said Sally. "We have to be in it."

It was Charlotte's voice that replied. "Don't bother. It's all more or less fixed up. The mounted followers are all going to be from here. People who keep their horses here."

"Don't tell me it's you again," raged Martine, coming toward them with a brochure and over-hearing Charlotte. "You would cause trouble in Antarctica! I don't want to know what was going on in the paddock to make Thalia take such a stupid risk—but I have no doubt you were the cause of it."

Charlotte hunched her shoulders and stomped away.

"Give that to your father." Martine handed Sally the brochure.

"Thanks," muttered Sally, wanting to escape.

"Never again, Thalia," warned Martine. "You only jump if I tell you to." Then she grinned suddenly. "But if you're interested in show jumping, I think that horse would take you to the top."

Thalia, who had been avoiding Martine's eyes, gave a gasping, choking gulp. Her face suddenly switched on like an electric light bulb.

"We'll see you both tomorrow morning," said Martine as they mounted.

"No," said Sally. "Our next lesson is the day after tomorrow."

"Lady Spencer's meeting. You must come and be mounted followers."

"Charlotte said—"

"Don't tell me you're still listening to things our dear Charlotte says?" demanded Martine. "She should be banned from coming here, the trouble she causes."

As they rode back to Kestrel Manor, their horses' hooves sharp on the road, Thalia was still beaming.

"I think she is the absolute best."

"Yes," agreed Sally. "Yes, she is." She squared her shoulders, looking straight ahead. "I'm going to practice my exercises sitting on the back of the sofa as well as when I'm riding."

"Why not?" agreed Thalia. If Martine had told her to practice jumping while standing in the saddle, she would have done it.

Chapter Four

W hen Sally got down to the stables the next morning, Thalia had already brought the horses in. She had groomed Tarquin, tacked him up, and was just starting on Willow with a dandy brush when Sally arrived.

"Late," stated Thalia.

"Mom burned the porridge. It was my turn to walk the dogs, and when I was all ready, Jamie spilled his orange juice on me. That's why."

"Don't talk, brush," said Thalia irritably.

When Willow was ready, Sally discovered that she had forgotten her hard hat and had to go back to her room at the top of the tower for it.

"We'd better ride along the beach," said Thalia when at last they were mounted. She led the way down the track to the shore. "It saves about ten minutes."

Whenever Tarquin's hooves touched the sand, he broke into a gallop. Willow followed. The sea wind blew back their hair and the brilliance of sea and wet sand dazzled their eyes. Sally urged Willow on, imagining herself riding in the pageant. They must reach Mr. Frazer's yard in time to be chosen as mounted followers.

As Sally galloped on, she gradually became aware of a noise behind her.

"Oh, please no. Oh no," thought Sally, not daring to look behind. "It can't be." But unless a wolf pack was pursuing them, it could only be . . .

Sally steadied Willow to a trot and forced herself to look back. It was.

Hurtling after them was Misty, her shaggy gray-and-white coat matted about her in wet, sandy strands of hair. She was running with her mouth wide open, the baying, barking, howling noise pouring out of it. Her round yellow eyes were staring at Sally.

Thalia reined Tarquin in and stared in horror as Misty caught up with them and flopped down in the sand.

"I must have left the door open," admitted Sally guiltily as she jumped off Willow. "Pretty good the way she tracked us."

"Good! The meeting starts in five minutes. We haven't got time to take her back to Kestrel Manor." Thalia gazed down in disbelief at the mound of hairy sand and the two yellow saucer-eyes glaring up at her.

"I suppose we'll have to take her with us," continued Thalia. "Perhaps we could shut her up somewhere, but if we don't get a move on, it will all be over."

"Why do you always have to be so bad?" Sally said to the Beardie. "Always you!"

Misty grinned and squirmed at Sally's feet, while Thalia found some binder twine in her jacket pocket. Sally knotted it onto Misty's collar as a makeshift leash. Misty, worn out by her pursuit, was dragged along unwillingly at the end of the twine.

To reach the stables, they had to ride through the sand dunes. The horses, high-stepping as hackneys, plunged their way upward to the road, while Misty burrowed her way along, with only her head visible.

When they reached the stables, there was nobody around, although the yard was blocked with cars.

"We can't leave them in a stall without asking," said Sally, loosening Willow's girth and easing her saddle.

Suddenly there was a burst of applause.

"That's them," said Thalia, pulling Tarquin toward the large sliding doors. "They're in here. This must be the indoor school." The doors were slightly open. Thalia peered in. At the far end of the indoor school were several rows of wooden chairs. Facing the audience were six more chairs occupied by two stout elderly men, one young man, and three formidable, horsey-looking women. As Thalia watched, the young man got up and began to introduce Lady Muriel Spencer.

"Lady Muriel," announced the young man, "is going to give us a rundown on her plans for the Torbracken Pageant."

"Let me see too," said Sally, trying to get closer to the crack between the doors. "What's happening?"

Just as Lady Muriel started to speak, Thalia managed to get her fingers around one of the sliding doors and give it an energetic push. The door swung back on oiled runners. Everyone in the indoor school looked around in surprise.

"Uh-oh!" exclaimed Thalia. She and Sally stood holding their horses like rabbits caught in the beam of headlights.

Martine Dawes jumped up and came running toward them.

"You're late," she said. "Lady Muriel's about to start. Bring your horses in and hold them. Really it would have been better if you hadn't brought them. My fault. Should have told you."

"Sorry," began Sally, when Martine gave a muffled gasp of horror.

"What on earth is that?" she exclaimed.

"Misty," said Sally.

Misty's matted, seaweedy coat had been sugared over with sand from the dunes. Her eyes were wide open and one of her special smiles lifted her lips from her pink gums, showing two rows of glistening fangs.

"She likes you," explained Sally. "She only smiles like that at people she likes."

"Are you going to sit down?" boomed Lady Muriel. "Can't possibly get going with all this interruption, don't you know?"

"Stay here," Martine said to Sally and Thalia. "You'll be able to hear okay." She sat down without closing the doors.

"Are we ready then?" said Lady Muriel. Sally retreated behind Willow, feeling that Lady Muriel was speaking directly to her.

Lady Muriel was about six feet tall and looked about seventy years old. She was wearing a bright green tweed jacket and plus-fours. Her bulletproof stockings were purple, and her brogue shoes and deerstalker hat looked older than Thalia's hard hat. Her weather-beaten cheeks were mottled scarlet, and her clear gray eyes gazed out imperiously. Her thin lips were a mouth-trap ready to snap.

"Now that I can make myself heard," said Lady Muriel, leaning on her stick, flashing lethal death-ray looks at Sally and Thalia. "I expect that you are all aware that a week from Saturday is open day at Torbracken and you are all going to attend. You are going to come and do your part, for everyone who comes and pays their three pounds' entry money will be striking a blow against the monstrous legions of woodworms that are burrowing their way through the very fabric of the west tower.

"We will defeat them," Lady Muriel went on, waving her stick in the air and rousing her audience to cheers.

"But first things first." Lady Muriel dived into her tweed pocket and brought out a long list written on what looked to Sally like scratchy toilet paper.

"Open all day," read Lady Muriel. "Refreshments in the dining hall, doors opening out onto the balcony, if the weather is dry. Craft stalls in the great hall—home baking, fortune-telling, paint a mug, stitch a tapestry, and many more anti-woodworm activities. Twelve o'clock in the walled garden, Scottish country dancing, archery demonstration, sheepdogs, yoga from the ladies in leotards and acrobatics from the Boy Scouts. Three o'clock the pageant begins. I have written it myself."

The sudden burst of cheering and clapping that followed made Tarquin dance his forelegs, clinking his bit, and Misty throw herself about at the end of her binder twine, barking furiously.

Lady Muriel continued. "When the lands and estates of Torbracken were granted by the king to the first Lord of Torbracken for his bravery in battle, there was very nearly a terrible mistake. Peter Brewer, an evil steward who had been left in charge of Torbracken House, tried to claim the honors for himself."

Lady Muriel's audience hissed and booed. Misty barked.

"When the king and his followers arrived, Peter Brewer stepped forward claiming to be the owner of Torbracken. He knelt before the king, waiting to be knighted, and at that very second the rightful owner returned from battle." Lady Muriel waved her stick over her head in triumph.

As the cheering died down, a tall, bespectacled man stood up.

"Lady Muriel," he asked, "would you give us some idea of when this took place? The historical setting, so to speak. Who was king?"

Lady Muriel's eyes sharpened to laser beams.

"My good man," she said. "I am telling you about a legend. I have no earthly idea who was king and to be quite frank with you I am not in the least concerned. In our pageant the Tarent Battlers are enacting our battle scene. I have given them an absolutely free hand. As long as there are pikes and swords and banners, I told them, that's all that matters."

The man sat down, totally squashed.

"Now, the first thing I want to get sorted out is the mounted followers. We need about twelve or so. Mr. Frazer has this in hand. You must all come without horses to the first rehearsal on Saturday and we'll work out a plan of action."

"That's us," said Thalia. "You hold Tarquin and I'll put our names down."

As Sally was about to take Tarquin, Lady Muriel waved her stick in the air again.

"I nearly forgot," she cried. "Anti-wood-worm weapon number one. The rightful lord is to be played by my great-nephew, Nick Ross."

A sudden flurry of surprise swept through the audience. Sally and Thalia looked at each other, not knowing what the fuss was about.

"Despite the danger of being called a doting old woman, I must say the *famous* Nick Ross. He is bringing his show jumper, Rose of Sharon, with him. I expect you will all have seen them show jumping on television."

For a long moment neither Thalia nor Sally could speak.

"*The* Nick Ross," croaked Thalia, getting her voice back first. "And Rose of Sharon! He is my favorite, my absolute and total super-favorite show jumper!"

"Mine too," echoed Sally. "The most."

"I've got posters of him all over my bedroom walls," stated Thalia.

"And we are going to ride in a pageant with him," said Sally.

"To ride with Nick Ross! To really see him riding Rose of Sharon!"

"Can't believe it," said Sally.

"It's true," said Thalia, and the whole of the indoor school sparkled and shimmered with the dazzle of rainbows.

Suddenly there came from the stable yard a banshee howling and barking. It was worse than a hundred fingernails being scraped down a hundred blackboards.

"Misty!" cried Sally.

Although she still had the binder twine securely wound around her hand, there was no disgustingly filthy dog at the other end.

Sally pushed Willow's reins at Thalia and dashed out into the stable yard.

"Misty!" she screamed. "Misty, come here!"

Misty hesitated, looked over her shoulder at Sally, and sprang into the muck heap, where she rolled luxuriously, still barking.

"Come here at once!"

Misty wriggled back to her feet and shook herself. She lifted one cautious paw and considered obeying Sally. In that instant another dog came bounding up.

He was a wolfhound puppy, Shetland-pony size but still a puppy. He had a rough, gray-brown coat, was beautifully groomed, and wore an expensive leather collar. The dog jumped up to dance circles around Misty, his front legs outstretched, his long thick tail wagging furiously as he bounded and bounced.

Sally stared in disbelief as the two dogs careened back to the yard. They raced in and out between the parked cars, having the time of their lives.

"Can't you catch her? They're all coming out," cried Thalia. "Martine's got the horses."

As the doors from the indoor school opened wider, the wolfhound leaped onto the hood of one car, then over another. Misty ran around the cars in desperate pursuit. People either stood staring or began chasing the dogs, making them more excited than ever.

"Surely that's Muriel's pup?" said a rich, fruity voice.

"Must be," replied her friend, "but where did the mongrel come from?"

"Collie—Bearded collie," said Sally automatically, but no one was listening to her.

Lady Muriel came through the doors into the yard. With one sweeping glare she took in what was happening. In a voice that would have stopped a waterfall in its course, she roared, *"Patrick!"*

The wolfhound puppy stopped in mid-leap, whipped around in the air, fled to his mistress, and lay down on his back at her feet.

"Car," commanded Lady Muriel. The puppy scrambled to his huge paws and slunk away toward an open sports car. He bounded in and lay in the back with his chin resting on the back of the driver's seat.

"Is that creature yours?" Lady Muriel demanded, pointing her stick first at Misty and then at Sally. "Remove it."

Misty arched her back, lowered her head and tail, and—moving very slowly—tiptoed her way across the yard to Sally.

"I'll kill you," promised Sally, knotting the binder twine to Misty's collar. "You are the worst—"

"Come on," interrupted Thalia. "We'd better get our names down to be mounted followers."

"Afraid you're too late," said Martine, giving them back their horses. "They picked the mounted followers just after you went off to find your dog. They only wanted a few. Nearly everybody will be foot followers. There's a rehearsal on Saturday at Torbracken. I should think your best plan would be to show up then. Two o'clock."

"Is Charlotte going?" asked Thalia, her voice shaky with disappointment.

"'Fraid she is. She's to be Nick's page."

Thalia and Sally looked at each other in total disgust.

"Go anyway," encouraged Martine. "But no horses. And it might be a good idea to leave your sand-hound behind."

Feet out of their stirrups, reins loose on their horses' necks, Sally and Thalia rode back across the beach to Kestrel Manor.

"We must ride in the pageant," said Sally. "Must."

"With Nick Ross and Rose of Sharon," breathed Thalia. In her mind there was no doubt. They would find a way of riding with Nick Ross.

Chapter Five

On Saturday, all the Lorimers except Meg and Misty, who were shut in the kitchen with three bones between them—because Misty always stole Meg's and three bones meant that there was always a spare one for Meg to move to—were driving between the beech trees from Kestrel Manor to the main road.

They were all going to the rehearsal at Torbracken House. Mr. Lorimer had found a pamphlet about the pageant at his library. It said that everyone who wanted to join in would be welcome.

Mr. Lorimer and Ben were hoping to join in the battle with the Tarent Battlers. Mrs. Lorimer had brought her watercolors, brushes, and sketch pad. She was intending to paint, and keep an eye on Jamie, who thought he was going to be a Battler with his father and Ben.

Sally was wearing her oldest jeans, scuffed tennis shoes, a black T-shirt, and her oldest jacket. It was camouflage. She and Thalia had decided that their best hope was to join in quietly with the unmounted followers. If nobody noticed them too much, maybe they would be allowed to stay.

Thalia was coming on the back of her narg's motorbike. Thalia's narg was also planning to be a Battler but, just as with Jamie, there probably wasn't much hope.

Torbracken House was not far from Kestrel Manor. It stood in an immensity of grounds—woodlands, formal gardens, fields of organically grown vegetables, and a walled garden where the pageant was to take place.

Boy Scouts were on duty. As Mr. Lorimer turned into the rhododendron-shaded drive, a Boy Scout directed them to the parking lot. When they got out of the car, more Scouts pounced on them, asking them which part of the pageant they were interested in.

"Soldiers through the woods to the left. The Tarent Battlers will tell you what to do. They are organizing the charge."

Mrs. Lorimer went off to be part of the general crowd.

"And you?" the Scout asked Sally.

"I'm not sure," said Sally, then heard the welcome roar of Narg's motorbike.

Thalia threw herself off the bike and came running across.

"Mounted followers," she said to the Scout, and he told them to go to the stable block behind Torbracken House.

"We're not really," said Sally guiltily as they walked under the sky-touching pine trees toward the stables.

"Of course we are," declared Thalia. "We are if they let us. We *must* ride with Nick Ross."

Already there were about fifteen people waiting by the stables, which were unoccupied and rather cobwebby.

"Look out," mouthed Sally. "Charlotte to your left."

"Take action," Thalia replied, and they edged their way around the yard until they found a place to wait, half hidden in a stall doorway, well out of Charlotte's sight.

"Here we are, here we are," chirruped a sharp, weaselly woman who came scooting into the yard. She had a cotton scarf tied over strawy hair, flat blue eyes, and a smile safety-pinned onto her face so you couldn't tell what she was really thinking.

"Let's get things straightened out. I've got all the information down here. When I call your name, please come over to me."

"Cut the cackle, Daisy," called a stout, purple-faced man.

"Rupert, do not start. Lady Muriel will be here in a jiffy. This is serious stuff. And she is in charge."

"Sorry, sorry. Only trying to cheer things up. My mistake."

"Right then," said Daisy, struggling to control the clipboard and sheets of paper she was carrying. "When I read out your name, please come over here. First, mounted followers in the battle—Sean McGregor on Mutant Turtle; Frank Gunn on Moly . . ."

Sally and Thalia looked at each other in despair.

"She won't call out our names," said Sally.

"Wait," said Thalia.

There were four groups of mounted followers. Those taking part in the battle, those who were with the evil steward, the king's followers, and the page who was to ride with Nick Ross—Charlotte.

"It should be us," muttered Sally.

"It will be," swore Thalia, but it was like vowing to swim the English Channel when you could hardly manage the length of the pool.

When Daisy had divided them all into their groups, she told them to stay where they were because Lady Muriel would be arriving at any moment.

"Bet she remembers me," said Sally uneasily.

With Patrick lolloping beside her, Lady Muriel surveyed her unmounted mounted followers.

"This way," she roared. "I shall show you where to ride when you have your horses. Everybody down to the walled garden." She marched ahead, rallying them on with a wave of her stick.

Sally and Thalia hung back.

"We'll be king's men," said Thalia. "They're the biggest group, so perhaps we won't be noticed."

Sally said nothing. A blind man on a runaway horse in a sandstorm would notice them.

Over the years the walls of the walled garden had crumbled away, and the stones lay moss covered and scattered. In some places the wall was only about three feet high. Broad flower beds stretched from the walls to wide lawns. Torbracken House was at one end of the walled garden. Formal paved walks and yew trees cut and shaped like strange creatures joined the house to the shaved perfection of the lawns. Outside the walls were several large chestnut trees.

"That's where the wretched worms are," Lady Muriel boomed, swinging her stick in the direction of the stone turrets and towers of Torbracken House. "In the west tower. But we'll sniff them out. We'll get them."

Sally shivered suddenly and got goose bumps. She felt sure that Lady Muriel would sniff her out. She glanced quickly at Thalia, but she was gazing around her, looking totally at ease, as if she had every right to be there.

First Lady Muriel lined up those who were to be in the battle, and then the steward's followers.

"Now the king's horses and the king's men."

Three men, two boys, and a lady began to walk across to Lady Muriel.

"Us too," said Thalia between her teeth.

For a moment Sally's feet would not move.

"Sally, come on," hissed Thalia. "We've got to be with them."

As she walked beside Thalia, Sally felt every eye boring into her. Almost before she heard Charlotte's voice, she knew it was going to happen, knew what Charlotte was going to say.

"Lady Muriel, those two girls in the back. They shouldn't be here. They weren't chosen." Charlotte's eyes shone with spiteful delight.

"We should be here," stated Thalia.

"Now, who told you to come? You're both far too young to be king's men," exclaimed Daisy.

"But Charlotte's young," said Thalia.

"Oh, but she is a page, dear," consoled Daisy. "You are not really mounted followers, are you? So come along with me and be part of the crowd."

Suddenly Lady Muriel pointed her stick straight at Sally.

"You are the child who brought that abomination of a mongrel to our meeting at the stables."

"Collie," corrected Sally. "Bearded collie. Purebred. Pedigreed."

"Out!" commanded Lady Muriel. "Away with you."

"But I haven't brought Misty—"

"Out," roared Lady Muriel again.

"I'll take them around to be part of the crowd," said Daisy. "Watching-the-dancing crowd, do you think?"

"We are not any sort of crowd," said Thalia.

"But of course you are, dear. Mounted followers were all specially picked, and we can't change anything now."

Daisy left them with the watching-the-dancing crowd.

"We're not staying here," said Thalia. "We've got to know what the king's men do, so when we bring Tarquin and Willow we'll know what to do."

"They'll only send us back again," said Sally.

She could see her father, Ben, and Thalia's narg charging around among the rhododendrons. Sally's mother was sitting on a garden seat painting, while Jamie, who had not been accepted by the Battlers, sat on the grass beside her eating chocolate.

"It's no good," said Sally.

"Of course it is. Don't be so soft."

Thalia led the way back to the walled garden. She and Sally crouched down behind the fallen stones from the crumbling wall, trying to see what was happening.

"Need to get closer," said Thalia. "Those are the king's men they're talking to now."

"You'll gallop along the drive," the man organizing the mounted followers was saying. "When you reach here . . ." and the man began to walk away, so Sally and Thalia couldn't hear him.

"Drat," said Thalia.

"They'll see us if we go any closer."

They both looked around, searching for a place to hide.

"The tree!" Thalia exclaimed. "They'll never see us there and we'll be able to hear everything."

Crouching as close to the ground as they could, the girls ran through the shrubbery to where a huge chestnut tree stretched its looping branches almost to the ground. It was an easy climb. When they had reached about halfway up, they each picked a branch and sat astride it, leaning against the trunk of the tree. They were completely hidden by the leaves but they could see everything that was happening in the walled garden.

"Listen hard," said Thalia, "so we'll remember. So we'll know what to do at the pageant."

Suddenly there was a banshee howl. Scrambling over the broken-down wall came Lady Muriel's wolfhound. He bounded across the grass and stood with his front paws on the trunk of the chestnut tree.

Lady Muriel came striding up behind him, one bony hand holding up her long denim skirt, the other waving her stick aloft. When she reached the chestnut tree, she walloped at its lower branches with her stick.

"I can see you," she cried, rousing birds from their treetops for miles around. "Get down at once! At once, I tell you!"

Sally and Thalia slid and scrambled their way out of the tree. They stood listening to Lady Muriel's raging, then made their way back to the walled garden.

"Crowd," said Sally bitterly. "That's all we are. Just crowd."

And for once Thalia had nothing to say.

Chapter Six

"*T*hat was much better," exclaimed Martine as Sally rode over the poles. "You were with your horse all the way."

Sally beamed, running her hand down Willow's smooth neck and patting her hard, fit shoulder.

It was their fourth jumping lesson, four days since their disastrous day at Lady Muriel's. Only three days to the pageant, and they were no nearer to finding a way of riding in it. Their only cunning, feeble plan was to arrive at Torbracken riding Tarquin and Willow and hope they would be allowed to join in.

"But no way if Lady Muriel and her hound of the Torbracken spots us," Thalia had said gloomily.

"Now Thalia," said Martine when she had altered the trotting poles to suit Tarquin's longer stride. "Your turn."

There were five trotting poles laid on the ground followed by a small jump. The horses had to trot rhythmically over the poles and then take the jump without changing their stride while their riders kept their jumping position.

"Steady. Drive him on with your seat, gather him together with your hands. Nice, good," encouraged Martine as Thalia rode toward the line of trotting poles.

Sally watched as Tarquin trotted over the poles, lifting his hooves cleanly between them and flipping neatly over the little jump. Sally could see how much he had improved. He had almost given up his wild dashing, and Thalia's aids had changed from sudden kicks into quiet, accurate instructions.

"Excellent," said Martine. "You have both been working hard at home."

"Trotting without stirrups," agreed Sally.

"Numb bottoms," said Thalia.

Suddenly one of the stable girls came running from the stables, waving her arms and shouting, "He's here. Nick Ross is here!"

"Bit early," Martine said, while Thalia and Sally gaped, wide-eyed and speechless.

"Right," said Martine, "we'll leave the jumping until your next lesson. I guess you'd like to meet Nick?"

"Oh, yes!"

"More than anything in the world!"

"Thought you might. You can put your horses into a stall for a few minutes," said Martine as she led the way up to the yard.

Parked in the stable yard was a brand-new, bright yellow, low-slung car. Attached to it was a trailer. As Sally and Thalia led their horses across the yard, there was a sound of trampling hooves from the trailer, followed by an ear-splitting whinny. The car door flew open and a young man jumped out.

"Rise and shine, Rosie," he shouted, banging on the side of the trailer.

He was tall, with curly black hair, very dark, glistening eyes, and a wide, smiling mouth. Sally and Thalia recognized him at once.

"It's him!" cried Thalia. "It is you, isn't it? Nick Ross? I never dreamed I'd ever see you like this. Just standing there."

"I do it quite often." Nick grinned. "Just stand, I mean."

"Oh, but not where I can see you," said Thalia. "When we heard you were coming, I counted all the pictures I've collected of you. I've got thirty-eight. Fourteen up on the wall and the rest in my show-jumper stall. You are my absolute favorite show jumper!"

"Continue," said Nick Ross, smiling down at Thalia. "Flattery will get you everywhere. Music to my ears."

"Put your horses in over there," said Martine, pointing to two empty stalls.

"And how is Martine?" Nick Ross asked, hugging her. "I only gave in to Auntie's nagging because it meant seeing you."

"Oh, really?" said Martine. She was flushed and bright, obviously delighted to see Nick Ross again.

Sally was just as thrilled as Thalia, but she kept her happiness to herself like a precious jewel that she didn't want to share with anyone else.

Willow and Tarquin watched curiously over their half doors as Nick Ross, speaking in a quiet voice, went into the trailer through the groom's door. The front ramp was lowered, and Rose of Sharon came down the ramp with Nick running at her side.

She stood in the yard—mighty, foursquare, pure white except for the black skin at her muzzle and eyes. She made everything around her seem second-rate, not worth having.

"She is looking well," said Martine. "Full of herself."

"So she should be. Won pots of money since you saw her last."

"She's like the Greek marble horses in the British Museum," said Sally.

"Winter and spring mixed together and made into a horse," exclaimed Thalia. "She is the most beautiful horse I have ever seen."

"She has brains as well," said Nick. "When you're sitting up there pounding up to a six-foot wall, it's not her looks you're thinking about, it's her brains. Isn't that right, Rosie, old girl?"

The great white mare crested her neck and blew over Nick's black hair.

"She's in love, like all the rest of your nags," said Martine, laughing.

"Well, of course!" said Nick. "Could we get her settled? Auntie Mu will be along any minute now. I phoned to let her know I was nearly here."

"Four-star service awaits you, Rosie," said Martine as Mr. Frazer came back from leading a ride.

"Guess we better not let Lady Muriel see us," said Sally.

"Phooey to her," Thalia said, and hurried after Nick Ross to watch him take off Rosie's bandages and traveling rug.

"Do you remember last year at the Horse of the Year Show when you just beat John Whitaker? That was because I had all my fingers crossed for you. If I think someone is going to beat you, I will them to knock down the jumps and they always do."

"So that's why I've been doing so well, is it? From now on I shall only jump in events that are being televised."

"If you'd let me know when you're jumping, I could sit at home and will you to win," offered Thalia.

"I'll consider your offer. How much would you charge?"

"Nothing!" cried Thalia, shocked at the very thought. "Nothing, of course."

Mr. Frazer came over to talk to Nick minutes before Lady Muriel tore into the yard in her scarlet sports car. She swung herself out of the car and ran across the yard. Pushing Thalia out of her way, she flung open the stall door and launched herself at Nick.

"So sweet of you . . ." she began, as Rosie

started back, rearing up and tossing her head before she plunged to freedom through the open stall door.

Nick struggled to free himself from Lady Muriel's embrace, but Rosie was already out of the stall and thundering across the yard.

It was Thalia who sprang at Rosie's head collar and held on with both hands, refusing to let go even when Rosie lifted her off her feet.

"Steady, lass," soothed Nick as he rushed to grab Rosie. "Whoa, old girl. Settle, settle."

Nick ran his hand down the mare's neck, patted her shoulder, and soothed her fright. Instantly she calmed down, gave a gusty sigh, and followed Nick back into the stall.

"Just like old times," said Lady Muriel cheerfully. "Never could tie up a pony properly. Always chasing after them down the drive."

"Good thing you were quick," Nick said to Thalia. "Or I'd be chasing Rosie down the road now. Thank you very much."

"So glad you made it," boomed Lady Muriel as Nick tied Rosie up securely. "Thousands will flock to my pageant just to see you. We will be hock deep in dead woodworms."

"That will make jumping difficult," said Nick, starting to groom Rosie.

"Tomorrow is the dress rehearsal. Quite wonderful the way everyone has rallied to the call. Cannot imagine what the lawn will be like after the Battlers have battled. But, as I said to Freddie, if we don't exterminate the wretched worms, they'll eat the house down."

Nick parked his brilliant yellow car and his trailer, spoke to Mr. Frazer, then ran across the yard and leaped into Lady Muriel's sports car.

She was just about to drive away when Nick turned around in his seat and shouted, "Nick Ross Fan Club, a word with you."

Sally had turned away, going to get Willow, but Thalia was still gazing after Nick. She raced toward the car. Nick spoke to her in a low voice, and the car drove away.

"What did he say?" demanded Sally.

"It's a secret."

"Go on," said Martine. "You can tell me."

"I can't, I promised."

Charlotte, who had just been dropped off at the stables by her mother, said, "Was that Nick Ross you were speaking to? What was he saying to you? You don't know him. Why would he want to speak to you?"

"Thank you for our lesson," Thalia said to Martine. Totally ignoring Charlotte, she went to get Tarquin.

"Okay," said Sally when they had reached the shore and were well away from the stables. "What did he say? I'm fan club too."

"He'll be schooling Rosie at seven o'clock tomorrow morning. *If* we're there, he said, we can watch. *If* we're there, he said, we can have a ride on her. *If* we're there, he said."

"What did you say?" asked Sally, filled with utter delight.

"I said, 'Nothing in the universe could stop me.'"

Chapter Seven

Sally and Thalia stood at the end of the indoor school and watched, entranced, as Nick schooled Rose of Sharon.

In the enclosed space she seemed enormous—a huge, soaring bulk of white horse. Her legs were power-packed pillars of strength, her body was large and hard as a tabletop, and her arching neck was crested like a stallion's. She had flat cheekbones, large ears, lustrous black eyes, and wide, scarlet-lined nostrils. Her mane was pulled and her tail fell in a thick cascade around her straight hocks.

When Nick had ridden her at a walk, trot, and canter, he worked on turns on the forehand and haunches; shoulder in half-passes, and reining back. Martine stood with Thalia and Sally explaining the various movements.

"He always was one for taking things slowly," said Mr. Frazer. "Pays in the long run."

Nick turned Rosie and rode toward them.

"Still favors her offside," said Martine.

"Dear Martine, only you would notice that," said Nick, grinning and leaping down from Rosie.

"Now, who's going first?" he asked, looking questioningly at Thalia and Sally.

Sally's heart tightened and a cold shudder ran down her spine. Since Thalia had told her that they were going to have a ride on Rosie, Sally had kept telling herself how lucky she was and how the loathsome Charlotte would give anything to ride Rosie. Now that the moment had come, though, Sally looked up at the height and power of Rosie and shivered nervously.

But Thalia was already cramming on her hard hat and bustling to be first.

Thalia spoke to Rosie. Then Nick gave her a leg up and adjusted her stirrups.

"Shall I walk with you?" asked Nick.

"Oh, no!" exclaimed Thalia. "That would make it a donkey ride."

"Take care then."

Cautiously at first and then with growing confidence, Thalia walked Rosie around the school.

"Change direction and let her trot on," called Nick.

Thalia rode across the school, then touched her heels to Rosie's sides and trotted. To begin with she bumped around, but soon she found her rhythm and managed to post. She rode with an ear-to-ear grin, sitting upright and looking straight ahead.

"Good," called Nick. "Now let Sally have her turn."

Sally gritted her teeth and swallowed hard. "Don't let them see that you're afraid," she told herself. "Because you're not. Sally Lorimer, you are about to ride a world-famous show jumper and all you're thinking about is being afraid. Stop it!"

Thalia sprang to the ground, landing lightly beside Rosie's shoulder. Her face was bright with achievement.

"When the queen says, 'Arise, Dame Thalia,'" she told Nick, "it will only be the second best thing in my life. This has been the best."

Clutching Rosie's saddle, Sally held out her leg and Nick tossed her up. If from the ground Rosie had seemed massive, from the saddle she seemed to Sally like a universe of horse. There was nothing else.

Nick shortened her stirrups, gave her the

reins, and, walking in front of Rosie, led the way around the school. Sally knew that they must be walking because they were keeping up with Nick, but it was like sitting on the elephant that she had once ridden at a zoo—you were moving but you hardly felt anything.

"Not quite what you're used to?" Nick asked, grinning up at her.

Sally thought of Willow and of Miss Meek's plodding ponies at the riding school where she used to ride when the idea of owning her own horse was no more than an impossible dream. She shook her head hard.

And yet . . . and yet . . . there was something familiar about riding Rosie. Something she just couldn't quite remember.

Nick stood back with Thalia and Martine, and Sally rode around by herself.

"Do you want to trot?" Nick called.

"Okay," Sally shouted back, hating her voice for sounding too high and shaky. She felt in her jacket pocket for a hanky, blew her nose, and put the hanky back. There was something small and hard trapped in the corner of her pocket. She felt it curiously, her fingers searching it. It was the unicorn.

"What trot?" said Thalia loudly.

Sally thrust the little unicorn back into her pocket. She squeezed her legs a fraction and had to grab up her reins as Rosie instantly broke into a trot.

Finding the unicorn when she had so completely forgotten about it was like being given an extra-special present when it wasn't Christmas or even your birthday. Sally's delight flowed down her reins and Rosie broke into a slow, flowing canter.

Sally was riding down the long side of the school and knew Rosie would stop when she reached Nick. So she sat still, enjoying herself, just sat there being carried smoothly along.

Suddenly Sally didn't want to stop. She touched her leg against Rosie's hard, fit side and sent her on around the ring for a second time and again for a third time.

"Hold it!" roared Nick. "That's enough of that! Bring her back here. Slow her down."

Sally tightened her fingers and instantly Rosie was trotting and then walking. As Sally rode her back to the others, she leaned over Rosie's withers, patting her shoulder, thanking her for a super ride.

"Thought you'd be taking her over the jumps next," Nick said in a not-amused voice as he reclaimed his horse.

"Sorry," said Sally, hardly knowing what it was that had made her canter Rosie. "She just cantered."

"Sure, sure," said Nick.

"But thank you," said Sally. "Thank you very much."

There was something plucking at her memory. A white horse that she had ridden before, a horse as powerful as Rosie and as gentle, as well-schooled and as obedient.

Nick remounted. When he had trotted around a few times he took Rosie over three jumps, which she cleared effortlessly.

"You are my best and only girl," Nick told her, patting her neck and slipping to the ground.

Sally and Thalia watched, still trying to find words to thank Nick properly, as he moved quickly and confidently around Rosie in her stall. He checked her over, groomed her, and, when he was satisfied, tipped a bucket of feed into her manger. Rosie chomped, syphoning it down.

"How about something to drink?" Nick asked them, and they followed him into a bright, modern kitchen.

Lady Muriel was there. She looked up when she saw Sally.

"Got that mongrel with you?" she demanded. "Don't bring it in here."

But Mrs. Frazer winked at the girls and said to Sally that she'd heard someone had been galloping Rosie around the school.

"I didn't canter," said Thalia, "because Nick didn't tell me to."

But Mrs. Frazer was giving them lemonade in mugs decorated with gnomes and leaves and nobody was listening to Thalia.

"Will you two be going to the rehearsal?" Nick asked. "Are you riding over?"

"No," said Thalia. "Mr. Lorimer is picking us up. We weren't chosen to ride."

"What's this?" Nick said to Martine. "Are the kids not riding in the pageant?"

"They are not," stated Lady Muriel.

"But surely you can fit two more in?"

"Absolutely not," said Lady Muriel. "And if they bring that wretched mongrel anywhere near Torbracken, they will be banned."

"Oh, really!" said Nick. "I could do with two more pages. Let them come?"

"Nicholas," said Lady Muriel. "Who is in charge here?"

"You are," said Nick, grinning, giving in.

"But we have ridden Rose of Sharon," said Sally to Thalia as they stood at the end of the lane waiting for Mr. Lorimer to pick them up and take them to the rehearsal.

"I know," said Thalia, "but we should be riding in the pageant. We should have been Nick's pages. We should. Now we'll probably never see him again."

Nick had been discussing his arrangements with Mr. Frazer and Lady Muriel. He was off to jump Gemini, one of his other horses, in a show, leaving Rosie at Mr. Frazer's. He'd be driving back very early on the morning of the pageant, probably arriving about seven. And after the pageant he was taking Rosie straight back home.

So Sally could see that Thalia was probably right. They really wouldn't see Nick or Rosie again. Only a glimpse of them at the pageant. Next time would be on TV.

"We should be riding in it," Thalia said again, refusing to be comforted. "We should, should, should!"

The Lorimers' car pulled up. It was over-loaded already with costumes, picnic fixings, all the Lorimers except the Beardies, and Thalia's narg.

"There's no room for you," said Mr. Lorimer, who had taken the day off. "But squeeze in. If the police see us, we've had it."

Mrs. Lorimer had shopping to do before she went to Torbracken, so Sally, Thalia, and Ben were dropped off at Torbracken's gates.

"I'll take my pike and my sword," said Ben. "I don't want Jamie messing around with them."

They walked slowly up the drive, not wanting to be too early. Along the way, Thalia told Ben how unfair it all was, and Sally imagined she was cantering along on Rose of Sharon.

Suddenly they heard the sound of trotting hooves coming along the road, sounding like a battalion of horses. The hooves slowed down and turned into the drive. As the sound came closer, Sally looked back. It was the mounted followers from Mr. Frazer's stables, just as she had known it would be.

They filled the whole drive, forcing Thalia, Sally, and Ben into the rhododendrons. At the back of the cavalcade was Charlotte on her piebald. She was talking to an older woman on a finely bred bay.

"That's her," Charlotte said in a loud voice, pointing to Sally. "It was only a tiny toss and she would not get on again. And now she seems to think she can barge her way into the stables and be in everything. Lady Muriel straightened her out."

They rode past, leaving Sally scarlet-faced and furious.

When they reached Torbracken House the Scouts took over. Battlers, dancers, foot followers, and crowd were swiftly sorted out. Sally and Thalia were sent to get their crowd costumes from a huge room in Torbracken House, where trestle tables laden with secondhand clothes mingled with suits of armor and dead animal heads hanging from the walls.

"Now, dears, are you specials?" asked a plump, white-haired lady in charge of one of the tables.

"We should be—" began Thalia.

"No," said Sally, past caring.

"Crowd, general," the lady said, and burrowed into the piles of clothes, coming out with floral skirts, which she belted around them, and patterned sheets, which she knotted around their shoulders as shawls.

"There," she said, setting a straw hat covered with wilting silken roses on top of Thalia's fizzing hair. "You'll come to the pageant wearing them and return them before you leave."

All afternoon the sun blazed down as Thalia, Sally, and some thirty others who were crowd shuffled around the walled garden. First they were to come out of Torbracken House to be crowd watching the dancing and singing, then they were to be terrified crowd watching while the battle raged. Next, sullen crowd muttering among themselves when the king almost knighted the wrong man. And last of all, cheering crowd when the true owner of Torbracken was knighted.

Three times Sally and Thalia slipped away to where they could hear the horses and Battlers being drilled by Lady Muriel and the organizing man. Twice they were spotted by Daisy, and the third time Lady Muriel threatened to ban them from the pageant altogether if she saw them again.

Thalia squared her shoulders and scowled up at Lady Muriel, ready to answer back. But Sally gripped her by the sleeve and pulled her away.

"If she bans us, we won't even see Nick at the pageant," Sally said, dragging Thalia away to be crowd again.

In the evening they rode their horses bareback along the beach, following the crimpling line of the waves.

"It is so unfair," mourned Thalia. "So unfair."

"I know," Sally agreed, but there did not seem to be anything they could do about it.

Chapter Eight

A ll night long Sally tossed and turned. In her dreams Charlotte stole Willow and rode her in the pageant with Nick. In her darkest nightmares Sally watched as Nick galloped Rosie around and around, leaping clean over Torbracken House. Lady Muriel followed, mounted on a black horse and cackling with evil laughter.

It was half past three when Sally woke completely. She sat straight up in bed, and for a second she could hardly think who she was. Then she remembered her last dream. It had been about the crystal unicorn.

Sally leaped out of bed, ran across to where her riding jacket was hanging behind the door, and searched through the pockets till she found the unicorn. She could not understand how she had forgotten about it again. Sitting on the window seat, her knees under her chin, her nightgown tucked under her toes, Sally looked quietly down at the glittering crystal unicorn, its green and scarlet eyes, its golden horn. Beyond the window gray sea stretched to gray sky. Only the unicorn in her hand glinted and shimmered.

"Unicorn, horn of light, show me the way." Sally spoke aloud, the words forming themselves, without her having to think them first.

And instantly Sally knew what she would do. She would go and wake Thalia and they would ride over to the stables to say good-bye to Rosie.

Sally scrambled into her clothes, crept downstairs, resisted the appealing eyes of the Beardies, and, once outside, raced down to the field.

Thalia was standing at the gate.

"How did you know?" demanded Sally, staring at Thalia in utter amazement.

"I woke up suddenly, and the only thing in my head was to go and see Rosie. I was coming to wake you."

"It was the unicorn," said Sally, taking it out of her jacket packet. "I was holding it in my hand and I just knew that I had to come and get you and ride to the stables."

Both girls stood staring down at the unicorn lying in the palm of Sally's hand. Then Tarquin came trotting to the gate and whinnied— breaking the spell.

"It's really very early," said Sally cautiously.

"So there will be no one to see us," said Thalia.

They rode along the beach, first trotting and then at a canter that changed to a gallop. It was as if something were forcing them on, as if they were riding on some urgent mission.

"But we're only riding to see Rosie," Sally thought, not knowing why she was crouching tight and close over her horse's withers, urging her on.

"I think there's a back way in," Thalia said when the stables came into sight. "If we go up onto the road, someone might see us."

Remembering Betsy and her foal and the noise the horses had made when they were ridden past her, Sally agreed. She followed Thalia around the fields toward the back of the stables.

There was no sound. The horses' hooves were muffled in the sand; there were no gulls' cries; there was no traffic on the road. It was far too early for anyone to be up.

"I think this is the place," said Thalia. She rode Tarquin across the scrubby ground to where a hawthorn hedge grew along the bottom of one of Mr. Frazer's fields. "Yes, this is it."

But Sally, riding behind Thalia, couldn't see a gate. There was a gap in the hedge, blocked with crossed poles, but no gate.

"I'll go first," said Thalia, and instantly Sally realized that she was going to jump the poles.

"You can't!" Sally exclaimed. "You can't! It's far too high."

"Don't be silly! We've jumped higher than that in the paddock. We're only jumping into the field. It's quite flat. Willow will clear it easily. Jump behind me."

"I can't," Sally began, pulling on Willow's reins, trying to hold her back. The crossed poles seemed enormous.

"Oh, stop," gasped Sally, but Thalia and Tarquin were cantering at the poles. Sally stared in total panic as Tarquin leaped, clearing the poles easily and landing far out into the field.

Willow's ears were up and her hooves trampled the ground as she danced to follow Tarquin.

"Come on!" called Thalia.

With a half rear, Willow bounded forward. Sally clutched at her mane, all of Martine's teaching totally forgotten. Willow raced at the jump, got in too close, and shot straight into the air, throwing Sally out of the saddle. When they landed, Sally fell forward onto Willow's neck. For a second Sally was sure she was coming off, but somehow, digging with her elbow into Willow's shoulder, clutching desperately at her fistful of mane, she managed to struggle back into the saddle.

"What did you do that for?" demanded Thalia scornfully. "You nearly fell off."

Sally was too angry with herself to answer. She knew it had all been her fault. If she had ridden Willow toward the jump, letting her canter on, remembering Martine's instruction to throw your heart over the jump, Willow would have jumped every bit as well as Tarquin.

"I think that's the stall Rosie is in," said Thalia as they rode along the side of a high hedge that led toward the stables. She pointed to a large stall standing a little way apart from the range of stabling.

Three oak trees grew at the end of the hedge, just in front of the gate. Thalia and Sally had almost reached the trees when they heard the sound of a heavy vehicle being driven into the stable yard. Sally looked at her watch. It was only twenty past four, too early for anyone to be up and around at the stables.

They halted and waited, hidden by the trees. To their surprise, the engine didn't stop in the stable yard but pulled up to the space in front of Rosie's stall.

Standing up in their stirrups, they saw a huge horse trailer with a Clydesdale horse painted on its side. Jumping down from the cab came two men. One was tall and angular with stooped shoulders, red hair, and a red beard. He looked around him with a shifty expression. His long nose sniffed the air as if he were searching for something, something that he intended to find no matter what the cost.

The other man was about twenty-five, unshaven, with dirty, fair hair and a blank expression. They were both dressed in shabby clothes. The older man had a dirty raincoat belted over tweed trousers, and the young man was wearing jeans, green boots, and an ancient tweed jacket that was torn and stained.

"What do they want?" Thalia mouthed.

Sally lifted eyebrows and shoulders to signal that she had no idea.

The men waited for a few minutes by the

trailer, talking quietly, then walked over to Rosie's stall.

"If they go in to Rosie I'll stay here, you go and get Mr. Frazer," Thalia said in an urgent whisper.

"Do you think they're going to steal her?"

Thalia nodded violently. Then, to their total amazement, Martine came from behind the row of stalls and hurried across the yard to the men. The three of them stood for a moment talking to each other. Then Martine went into the stall and the two men let down the ramp of the trailer.

"Go and get Mr. Frazer," mouthed Thalia.

"Can't. Not when it's Martine, too."

In minutes Martine had led Rosie out of her stall and into the horse trailer. The ramp soared skyward, shutting her in. The two men and Martine climbed into the cab, and the trailer was driven out of the yard.

"Where are they taking her?" demanded Sally. "Nick's coming for her here on the morning of the pageant. Why have they taken her away?"

"They've stolen her," said Thalia.

"Not Martine!"

"You saw her. She's in on it too. A show jumper like Rosie would be worth thousands of pounds."

"But Martine wouldn't do a thing like that."

"We just saw her. Come on, we've got to follow them. Find out where they're taking her."

"We'll never catch up with them."

"It's Mr. Stamford's horse trailer. He uses Clydesdales on his farm. Bet they're taking her there. Come on, it's not too far from here."

Thalia jumped off Tarquin, opened the field gate, and in no time they were cantering along the road to Stamford's farm.

"This way," called Thalia. They turned down a track that led along the edge of a field of crops and looped around a hill of rough grazing. In front of them was a low-lying farmhouse cushioned in sycamore trees. They skirted around the hill until they could see the back of the farm. There in the yard was the horse trailer.

"If anyone comes out, they're bound to see us," said Sally. Her imagination was filled with visions of the red-bearded man and the fair-headed man pouncing on them, dragging them off their horses, and leaving them bound and gagged before taking Rosie away, never to be seen again.

They rode downhill toward the farm and had just reached the shelter of a high stone wall when they heard voices. Jumping down from their horses, they each found a spy hole between the stones.

"He'll never find her there," said the red-bearded man.

"Never," laughed Martine.

"That'll teach him," agreed the younger man.

Through her spy hole Sally was just able to see Martine closing the top door of a stall on Rosie and turning to walk away with the two men, back to the farm.

"They *have* stolen her," whispered Thalia. "Bet they don't leave her here for long. She'll be on a plane tonight. They'll probably take her to America or sell her to some Arab sheik."

"But not Martine," Sally protested.

"Come on, let's go in and speak to Rosie," said Thalia, ignoring Sally. "We've got to let her know we're here."

They knotted their reins over their horses' necks and left them by the side of the wall. Then they climbed over a gate, made a frantic dash across the yard, opened the stall door just wide enough to let themselves in, and quickly shut it again once they were inside. Tight with nerves, they waited to see if anyone had seen them, but there was no sound of footsteps or voices.

Rosie pricked her ears, lowered her great white head, and blew over their hair.

"It's all right," said Sally, stretching up to pat Rosie's neck. "Nick will be back tomorrow. We'll tell him where you are."

"Don't be so stupid," hissed Thalia. "We can't leave her here! They'll be back for her. Think of Shergar. Someone horsenapped him and nobody ever saw him again."

"We could tell my dad."

"And he'd tell the police, and then what would happen to Martine?"

Dust motes danced in a beam of light from a window high in the roof. The good smells of hay and horse filled the air. Rose of Sharon loomed above them, huge and white in the gloom.

"We've got to do something," said Thalia desperately. "And we've got to do it now."

"Take her to Kestrel Manor," said Sally, for it was the only way, the only way they could be sure of keeping Rosie safe for Nick.

Chapter Nine

"At last!" exclaimed Thalia. It seemed to have taken them ages to put on Rosie's tack. Every second they had been sure that someone would come in and find them.

"Kestrel Manor, here we come."

For a second they hesitated.

"What if they catch us?" Sally thought. "What if someone sees us before we get home? What would Dad say? Would the police think we'd stolen her? What if she gets away and causes an accident or injures herself?"

But Thalia had already taken the reins over Rosie's head and was opening the stall door.

"Shut it behind us," Thalia said as Rosie burst out of the stall into the yard.

She stood staring about her, a massive mountain of horse. Her crested neck and bulked shoulders were high above Thalia's head as Thalia led her across the yard, through the gate, and into the field.

When Rosie saw Tarquin and Willow, she

whinnied with a sound of thunder and the two smaller horses came trotting toward her. Tarquin gave sharp pig-squeals of delight as Rosie, dragging Thalia behind her, stormed to meet him.

"Catch him," yelled Thalia. "Get them away from Rosie. I can't hold her!"

Sally grabbed the reins of both horses.

"Come on," she urged, running ahead and trying to drag the horses with her. "Leave Rosie alone. Come on!"

Willow trotted obediently forward, but Tarquin, half-rearing, fought to get to Rosie. Grasping both reins, Sally was stretched out between the two horses while Thalia hung on to Rosie's reins with both hands.

"I can't hold her!" Thalia screamed desperately.

Sally swung Willow around. Yelling and hauling at Tarquin, she managed to drag them both off the track and into the field.

"It's no good," shouted Thalia, who was still anchoring Rosie by hanging on to her bit ring. "You'll have to ride them."

But when Sally rode Willow and led Tarquin it wasn't any better. Twice Tarquin dragged his

reins out of Sally's grasp and trotted back to
Rosie, trapping Thalia in a fury of stamping
hooves and reaching teeth.

The second time Thalia managed to drag
Tarquin away from Rosie and give his reins
back to Sally, she was close to tears.

"We can't go on like this," she told Sally.
"Someone's going to get hurt. I don't want
Tarquin kicked and lamed, even if it is by a
world-famous show jumper." She glared at
Rosie, almost hating her.

"Could I take Rosie?" Sally suggested.

"Might as well try. We must get back to
Kestrel Manor before there are any cars on the
road or someone is bound to see us."

In a tangle of reins they changed over. In
minutes Thalia had mounted Tarquin and,
heels sharp against his sides, hands hard on his
reins, had him paying attention to her while
Willow walked mildly at his side.

Grasping Rosie's reins, Sally followed
behind, the mare high-stepping at her side.
Rosie's neck was arched and she clinked her bit
impatiently, shaking her head against Sally's
feeble hold.

They were almost around the hill when a

hare leaped up at Rosie's feet. Rosie sprang to the side, rearing, dragging Sally off her feet, then leaped forward, blundering into Tarquin and Willow. Tarquin bucked furiously, dumping Thalia onto the ground.

Sally felt Rosie's reins scorching through her hands. And then Rosie and the two other horses were free.

In seconds all three of them were hightailing it over the hill while Sally stood blowing on her hands and Thalia struggled to her feet.

"Come on!" screamed Thalia. "We've got to catch them before Rosie breaks a leg."

At top speed they raced over the hillside to where the three horses stood watching them. They had almost reached them when Tarquin flung up his heels and galloped back toward the farm, the other two following close behind. Again Sally and Thalia raced after them. And again Rosie and the others stormed off over the hillside just as the girls got close.

"It's no use," cried Thalia. "We'll never catch them this way. Never!"

"Someone's bound to come out and see us," said Sally. "We've got to catch them."

"We'll walk backward," said Thalia. "When

they see our backs, they'll think we're going away from them."

Stumbling over the rough ground, the girls approached backward. Rosie, Tarquin, and Willow stood with their heads low, ears pricked, staring suspiciously at this strange behavior.

"When I say 'now,' we turn and grab," mouthed Thalia.

They walked backward until Sally was certain they were going to bump into the horses.

"Are you ready?" demanded Thalia.

Sally gulped and nodded.

"Now," breathed Thalia.

They sprang around and flung themselves at the horses, but they were far too slow. With Rosie leading, the horses plunged away.

"We'll never . . ." began Sally.

"We've got them," screamed Thalia, and raced toward the horses.

As they galloped off, Tarquin's stirrup had become entangled with Willow's stirrup leather. Both horses were standing stock-still, neither able to understand what was holding them back. Even when Sally grasped Willow's reins and Thalia closed her hand on Tarquin's bridle, they did not move.

Quickly Thalia untwisted the stirrups.

"You are the most foul, horrendous horror," she told Tarquin in tones of loving kindness.

"But Rosie?" asked Sally anxiously.

"Perhaps she'll follow them," said Thalia hopefully.

They turned and led their horses away. Rosie, with a trumpeting whinny, came stamping after them. Her front feet thundered the ground as she reared beside them. Sally felt Rosie's reins swing against her arm, and grabbed. For a second the white mare plunged backward, almost pulling Sally off her feet. Then Rosie stood still, blowing through wide nostrils.

"Whew," Thalia breathed. "Thought you'd had it."

They stood staring at each other, knowing that anything could have happened to the horses in their mad galloping.

"What are we going to do now?" asked Thalia desperately. "How are we ever going to get back to Kestrel Manor? They can't carry on like this on the road."

"You could ride Rosie," said a voice in Sally's head, and at once she knew why Rosie had seemed so familiar. One of Sally's dream horses before she found Willow had been Lucia—a white mare as proud and as powerful as Rose of Sharon. That was why she had wanted to canter Rosie; that was why she had not been afraid.

"I'll ride Rosie," said Sally. "You'll need to give me a leg up."

"You can't! Not on the road! She might run off with you. She could rear or shy or anything."

"She won't," said Sally. "She knows me. Honestly, we'll be okay."

Because she couldn't think of anything else to do, Thalia agreed and gave Sally a leg up. Pulling at the saddle, Sally scrambled astride the white mare.

"We'll go first," Sally said when she had straightened out her stirrups.

And hardly giving Thalia time to get on Tarquin, Rosie broke into a drumming trot.

Sally made no attempt to hold her back. She had never checked Lucia, and now she let Rosie have her head. They cantered up the path by the cornfield. When they reached the road, Rosie turned willingly in the direction of

Kestrel Manor and cantered along the grassy shoulder.

There was nothing in Sally's world but the power of her dream horse, now real in the form of Rose of Sharon.

As they approached Kestrel Manor, Sally tightened her reins and Rosie bumped into a trot and then a walk. Sally rode her through the gateway and waited in the drive for Thalia to catch up.

"You went like lightning!" cried Thalia. "If Nick could have seen you! These two are exhausted."

Seeing Willow blowing and sweating made Sally suddenly conscious of the real world again.

"Better get Rosie into a stall," said Thalia, and Sally walked her down the drive toward the black tower of Kestrel Manor. Now it was Rose of Sharon she was riding; Lucia had vanished.

There was still no sign of life at home. Even Misty did not bark when they passed the house on their way to the stables.

When they had settled Rosie, giving her water and hay, they shut the top half of the stall door on her. They rubbed down their own horses and left them in their stalls, afraid to turn them out in case Rosie made a fuss about being left alone.

"Now what?" demanded Thalia.

"Food," said Sally. "We'll have a picnic out here to avoid questions."

There was no one in the kitchen, so Sally searched through the cupboards and returned to Thalia with bread, butter, cold cheese-and-potato pie, half a bowl of Jell-O, and lemonade.

But even when they'd eaten, things weren't any better.

"One thing is certain," said Thalia. "We've got to keep her here until Nick comes back tomorrow."

"What if they come looking for her? Martine and those two men?"

"They would never think of coming here," stated Thalia with total optimism.

"But what if the police come?"

"I bet you they won't have gone to the police. That's the last place they would go. It's your parents who we have to keep from seeing her."

"Usually they only come down in the evening to check that everything is all right. Maybe they won't notice."

Later, when Sally and Thalia went into the
house, Sally asked her mother if Thalia could
stay the night.

"Of course, if it's okay with Narg," said Mrs.
Lorimer, her head full of plans for the pageant:
costumes, food, Jamie (who was not being
allowed to be a Battler and had to be amused),
Beardies, and Mr. Lorimer's sword—which still
had to be made.

"We thought we would keep the horses in, so
they'll be clean for tomorrow. I know we can't
ride them in the pageant, but we might just ride
them *to* the pageant and we'd want them to
look perfect."

"As long as you don't cause any more
trouble with the old lady," said Mrs. Lorimer.

"We won't," said Sally vaguely.

Thalia went to ask her narg if it would be all
right if she stayed with Sally. Sally washed up
and tidied her room. Quickly she twitched her
things away into drawers and closet. She settled
her comforter onto her bed, threw herself down
on top of it, and thought, "We have Rose of
Sharon in our stable. I rode her here." She shivered with delight. But there wasn't time to lie
and daydream about it. Sally jumped back up

and raced down to the stables to listen outside Rosie's door and make sure she was still there.

When Thalia came back, they groomed their horses, though their plan of riding to the pageant in the hope of joining in was forgotten. Nothing mattered now except to let Nick know that they had his show jumper.

"Tell me again," said Thalia when they were both sitting in the yard cleaning their tack, "the exact words you heard Nick saying to Mr. Frazer."

"I've told you about ten times already and you must have heard him yourself," Sally said, but that did not stop her from going over it again. It seemed the only thing worth doing to fill in the minutes that lumbered past like hours. "Nick said he would be driving up first thing tomorrow morning. He would go straight to Mr. Frazer's and that he expected to be there about seven."

"We've got to stop him from getting there," said Thalia. "We've got to catch him and tell him that Rosie is safe."

Morning crept into afternoon.

"Whatever happens, we must catch Nick before he reaches the stables. If he finds Rosie isn't there, he will go straight to the police. Then what would happen to Martine?" Sally repeated for the umpteenth time.

Every hour on the hour they went in to see Rosie, to fill up her water bucket and give her more hay.

"Hope this is right," said Sally as she filled the hay net again.

"Won't matter for one day. It's not as if it's oats. Nick can sort it out tomorrow."

"If we catch him," said Sally as they left Rosie alone again. She stood placidly dozing, paying no attention to Tarquin roistering around in the next-door stall.

In the evening only Ben came to tell them it was time to go in and to ask if the horses were all right. He was far too excited at the thought of being a Battler to notice the closed stall door or hear the sound of heavy hooves on the stone floor.

When they went up to bed Thalia said it would be best if they sat up and kept their clothes on for the morning, so that whenever the alarm went off they would be ready. Sally agreed and set the alarm for five o'clock so they would be certain to be at the crossroads at six.

After an hour of sitting up, it seemed more sensible to lie down under the comforter. In a few moments they were both asleep.

The alarm rang at five, making Sally turn over and Thalia hide her face in the pillow, but neither of them woke up.

Chapter Ten

*I*t was Misty who woke them, scratching at the door to get in.

"Half past six," screamed Thalia, grabbing Sally and shaking her awake. "We'll be too late for Nick."

Still drugged with sleep, they staggered into the bathroom, then pulled on jodhpur boots, grabbed up hard hats, and hurtled downstairs, banging the back door in Misty's face.

They had hardly arrived at the crossroads when Nick's brilliant yellow car scorched toward them.

"Nick, *stop!* Nick Ross, *stop! Stop! Stop!*" they screamed, standing up in their stirrups, waving wildly, ready to gallop after Nick if he didn't stop.

The car roared past them. Then, with a screech of brakes, it skidded to a halt.

"What the dickens are you two doing now?" demanded Nick, sticking his head out the car window and watching in blank amazement as

Sally and Thalia rode down upon him, both shouting at once.

"They tried to steal her," gasped Thalia. "But we stopped them. We saved her."

"She's at Kestrel Manor. She's safe. We rescued her for you."

When Nick had calmed them down and managed to make out that Rosie was at Sally's house, he said he would drive on and meet them there. Then they could explain exactly what had happened.

When Sally and Thalia reached Kestrel Manor, Nick had parked halfway down the drive.

"Follow us," said Sally. "And could you be as quiet as possible? My family doesn't know about Rosie."

"I hope you kids have got a good explanation for all this."

"They were stealing her," said Thalia. "And *we* saved her for you."

Nick started to ask another question but changed his mind. "Right. Let's go," he said impatiently.

Sally and Thalia led the way past the house and around to the stables. They jumped off their horses and rushed them into their stalls. By the time they had shut them in, Nick was in with Rosie—patting her, talking to her, and checking her over to see if anything had happened to her.

"Now," he said, looking up sharply. "Let's have it."

"They were stealing her—" began Thalia.

"Who?" interrupted Nick.

"Two men," said Sally, and sent a dagger look at Thalia warning her not to mention Martine. "They took her to Stamford's farm. We followed them and brought Rosie here."

"If it hadn't been for us, she might have been in America by now," said Thalia, who thought Nick was not being as grateful as he should have been.

"Stamford's farm?" asked Nick. "And what did the two men look like?"

"One had red hair and a red beard and was tall and round-shouldered. The other had fairish hair and was young," said Thalia.

"I thought as much," said Nick, and suddenly he was roaring with laughter. "The bad old rascal. And I'll bet you Martine had a hand in it too!"

"What's so funny?" demanded Thalia.

"Because . . ." began Nick, but couldn't speak for laughing. "Because . . ."

"I don't think it's funny," said Sally. "You might never have seen Rosie again."

"Sorry," gasped Nick. "I might have known they'd be up to something. Listen, your thieves were Lady Muriel's son and grandson."

"They couldn't have been!" exclaimed Thalia. "They were real villains and filthy dirty. You should have seen them."

"But that's who they were. Their idea of a joke. Snatch Rosie. Wait for me to arrive back. No Rosie. Thomas, that's the grandson, would have taken my place in the pageant, which was what he wanted to do. When I was over at Torbracken, he was moaning on about being the rightful heir and how *he* should be in the pageant, not me."

"You mean it was all a *joke*? Rosie was safe all the time?" demanded Thalia, hardly able to believe what Nick was saying.

"It wasn't easy rescuing her," said Sally. "And all the time she didn't need rescuing."

"Oh, but she did!" exclaimed Nick. "Now that we've got her here, we can show them what's what. They must have been going crazy trying to phone me to tell me that Rosie had vanished. But they weren't able to get me because I changed my plans, stayed at a different place."

"Are you going to tell them you've found her now?" asked Thalia.

"Absolutely not. I am going to phone Auntie Mu. No one will be up, so I'll leave a message on her answering machine telling her that I've been delayed and asking that they bring Rosie to the pageant. Of course they won't be able to because she's here, so—panic, panic, panic. But the pageant will go on. I'm certain Thomas will be geared up to take my part. So we are going to ride over, wait hidden in the pine trees until we get a signal that the battle is over and the evil steward has been done in. Then, as the king is about to knight the real owner—played by Thomas—we will gallop into the walled garden, expose Thomas for the rascal he is, and claim Torbracken as ours!"

"We?" demanded Thalia. "You and Rosie?"

"Thought you were both desperate to ride in the pageant. Or have you changed your minds?"

"Of course we want to ride in it!" exclaimed Thalia.

"You mean we can ride with you?" cried Sally.

"Must have pages. Can't be a rightful owner without two pages." Nick went out to his car to phone Lady Muriel.

"All fixed," he said, coming back to them. "Message left on the answering machine. Total confusion will follow." Nick patted Rosie, pulling her long ears through his hands, chuckling in delight.

"Wait till Charlotte sees us," said Thalia, gloating at the thought.

"Now, might your parents oblige with some coffee? Then I'll exercise Rosie and we'll make our plans."

When Nick had been introduced to the Lorimers, finished his coffee and toast, and gone out to Rosie, Mr. Lorimer gave Sally and Thalia a hard look.

"Perhaps," he said, "there is a little explaining to be done about your part in all this. Why didn't you tell us about it?"

"We couldn't," said Sally. "In case you told the police and they accused Martine."

"We were sure they'd stolen Rosie. It was not funny then," declared Thalia.

"You *should* have told us," said Mrs. Lorimer. "We'll discuss it later. Did Nick say you'd need costumes?"

"Sort of tabards to wear on top of our shirts, and cloaks?"

Mrs. Lorimer said she had not a second to spare, that they all had to be at Torbracken at one o'clock, but that she would see what she could do.

While Nick was exercising Rosie, Sally and Thalia groomed their horses and gave their tack a quick going-over.

When Nick came back, they all sat down around the kitchen table.

"Listen carefully," said Nick, grinning at everyone. "This is it: Sally and Thalia and I will ride along the back lanes to Torbracken. We'll go in through the farm and wait at the edge of the pine trees. The pageant starts at three, doesn't it?"

"Yes," said Ben. "That's when I'm on. There are peasants and servants from the house watching the dancing, and then it's the battle."

"Could you slip away whenever the battle starts and come and let us know as fast as possible?"

"Easy," said the newest member of the Nick Ross Fan Club.

"Perfect!" said Nick. "So there's the battle, and then the king and his mounted followers return to knight the owner of Torbracken House. He nearly knights the evil steward, but just in time Thomas will ride in as the real owner of Torbracken. That's when we must gallop in through the formal gardens, just before he is knighted. I shall give that Thomas what for! I'll teach him to lay a finger on my Rosie."

"You'll need to get your timing just right," said Mr. Lorimer. "No use if Thomas is knighted before you arrive."

"Don't worry, we'll be there." Nick laughed and sprang to his feet, waving an imaginary sword around his head.

It wasn't until Sally was tying her red-velvet curtain-cloak around her shoulders that she felt her stomach tighten with nerves. It had all been so sudden, changing from riding Willow to the pageant knowing that they were bound to be turned away, into riding there with Nick and Rosie to show that Nick was better than them all, that no one could trick him and get away with it.

Running across to the stables with Thalia, Sally stopped dead, whirled around, and raced back to her room. She snatched up the crystal unicorn and buried it deep in the pocket of her jeans.

When she reached the stables, Nick was mounting Rosie. He was wearing long, soft-leather thigh boots, purple hose, a gold-and-scarlet waistcoat over a white shirt, and a black cloak.

"The game's afoot," he cried, rousing them on. "We'll show them!"

When they reached Torbracken, they waited, holding their horses in the shelter of the pine trees.

"It's twenty past three," said Nick, looking at his watch uneasily. "Thought your brother would have been here by now. Better get up."

They mounted and rode to the edge of the pines. From Willow's back Sally could see the Torbracken grounds, tea being served in the courtyard, six sheep in a pen, a group of archers carrying their targets, and farther away, the crumbled-down walls of the walled garden. But there was no sign of Ben.

"Nearly half past," said Nick. "Even Auntie Mu's timing couldn't be as bad as this."

Suddenly Sally saw Ben. He was running full tilt toward the pine trees.

"Here he is," yelled Thalia, pulling up her girth. Sally eased her hard hat on. Suddenly her stirrups felt hopelessly uneven.

"Couldn't get away," Ben gasped. "You need to go *now*. Quick. At once. Or you'll be too late."

Not waiting for Ben to finish, Nick cantered Rosie out onto the lawns. He rode her as if she were a snowplow, sweeping people away before him. Sally and Thalia rode in his wake.

"Got to get there in time," Thalia muttered, sending Tarquin flying after Rosie. "Got to show them that Nick is best."

They came to a rise in the land and could just see down into the walled garden. Thomas was dismounting from a bay horse. Charlotte, holding her own piebald's reins in one hand, was ready to take Thomas's reins in the other. The evil steward lay on the ground apparently dead. The king held his unsheathed sword in his hand.

They were too late. There was absolutely no

way they could ride around through the formal gardens before Thomas was knighted.

"Need to jump," cried Nick. "Can you make it?"

"Of course," yelled Thalia, tightening her reins, making Tarquin dance, spring-heeled, ready to jump the moon.

Sally gazed terror-stricken at the wall. Fallen stones lay in mossy heaps on the side facing them, and she knew that on the other side were more cascades of stone and the breadth of the flower border. She remembered how she had nearly fallen off when she had jumped into Mr. Frazer's field.

Never could she jump it. Never. Never. She longed to shout, "No! No! It's too high, too broad. I'm not jumping it." But her mouth was frozen. The words weren't there.

"Keep behind me and jump where I jump," Nick shouted, standing up in his stirrups. For a moment he looked back over his shoulder, bright and fearless, tossing down his challenge to Thalia and Sally, daring them to follow where he led.

And as if there was some sort of electricity about Nick, a force that energized her whole being, Sally stopped being afraid. She remembered the unicorn in her pocket.

Sally saw Nick gather Rosie together, was aware of astonished faces staring up at them, saw Rosie pound her hooves into the earth and rise like a snowstorm, soaring over the fallen stones, rising over the wall.

"Right," breathed Thalia. "Keep together."

And there was no thought in Sally's head except to follow Nick. Martine's voice clear in her head, she paced Willow toward the wall and felt without hesitation the exact moment when Willow took off. Almost without knowing it, she bent her waist, going with her horse. She felt Willow rise, soar, and stretch out, saw Thalia land at her side and Nick already galloping across the walled garden.

It was like the moment when you knew you could swim or ride a bike. Sally knew she could jump.

Nick pulled Rose of Sharon to a rearing halt. The king's uplifted sword fell to the ground.

"Nick!" gasped Thomas from where he knelt in front of the king. "How did you get here? Where did you find Rosie?"

"Avaunt, you scullion," roared Nick, making Rosie rear again. "Foul varlet! Squalid thief! I have you now." Leaping down from Rosie, Nick drew his sword and raged at Thomas.

Thomas lifted his arms to protect his face, shouting at Nick to stop it, that it had all been a joke.

"Joke? I'll give you joke!" Nick thwacked Thomas with the flat of his sword until he struggled to his feet and ran up the middle of the walled garden, caught his foot on a hoofprint and fell facedown on the grass.

Nick grabbed him up and threw him over Rosie's withers. Then, jumping onto Rosie, he galloped around the garden waving his sword above his head.

The people watching cheered and clapped, demanding a second lap of honor, which Nick triumphantly took.

"You're next," Thalia threatened Charlotte. "Apologize to Sally. Promise you'll stop that stupid giggling."

Charlotte hesitated, saying nothing.

"Go on," said Thalia. "Apologize now, or else . . ."

As Nick came galloping back, still holding Thomas securely across his saddle, Charlotte stammered out an apology.

"I—I'm sorry. I—I didn't mean to say anything. I won't giggle again. I won't laugh or anything like that."

"Remember that," said Thalia. "Because Nick will be coming back and he'll deal with you."

When everything was over, Sally and Thalia, because they were with Nick, found themselves in the courtyard in front of Torbracken House. Battlers, followers, archers, sheep and sheep-dogs, and crowds of all kinds were making their way home, and Lady Muriel was serving champagne to family and friends.

"Lemonade for the kids," requested Nick, ignoring Thalia's suggestion that they would not object to champagne.

"Well done, everybody. Jolly well done, I say. This day has brought destruction to all wood-worms. Thanks to you all," said Lady Muriel.

Nick, Thomas, his red-bearded father, the organizing man, Martine, and several other helpers raised their glasses.

"And to Nick," squeaked Sally, completely carried away by the occasion.

"Have you forgiven us?" Martine asked Nick. "Thomas was desperate to have your part. He wanted to be knighted and to be the real owner, which after all he will be someday. I could see it was a bit unfair. Just because you're famous and were bound to draw the crowds."

"It was too much," said Nick.

"It was meant to be a joke. We wanted you to arrive. No Rosie. Thomas would need to take your part."

"And what if I'd gone to the police? Which I would have done immediately."

"We were going to say that we'd already told the police and that there was an officer coming to see you at the pageant. Of course there wouldn't have been, but after Thomas had been knighted we were going to bring Rosie on as lost property and make you pay a fine to get her back."

"I am not amused. Under my smiling face I am furious about the whole thing. Bet you were all going crazy when you found she'd vanished."

"You could say that, but that would be putting it mildly. We couldn't reach you on the phone. We didn't want to involve the police in case the newspapers got hold of the story. Lady Muriel calmed us down. Said she was sure you were at the bottom of it and the best thing we could do was wait until you arrived."

"Of course, all Auntie Mu was thinking about was her pageant," said Nick.

"Could be," agreed Martine. "But you'll never know how relieved I was to see you jumping over that wall on Rosie."

"I can imagine," said Nick, grinning.

Thomas's father came up and began to apologize to Nick, and Mrs. Lorimer came searching for Sally and Thalia. Meg and Misty bounded at the end of their leashes. Someone had brushed out their coats until they looked like show dogs—pure white ruffs, paddy paws, black and gray coats, shining cascades of silken hair.

"Like your dogs," said Lady Muriel. "What breed?"

"It's Misty," said Sally in delight. "And Meg. I've told you before. They are purebred, pedigreed Bearded collies!"

Lady Muriel snorted in disbelief.

"Time you were getting home," Mrs. Lorimer said. "We're going, so don't be long."

And suddenly Sally realized that it really was all over. They had ridden in the pageant with Nick Ross, the world-famous show jumper, and Rose of Sharon, his snow-white mare. And she knew how to jump. Knew what they meant when they told her to bend her waist. But it was over.

Nick said he had to be going soon. He made arrangements to leave Rosie at Torbracken while he went with Thomas's father to collect his own car from Kestrel Manor and his trailer from Mr. Frazer's stables. Then, after promising Sally and Thalia tickets for the Horse of the Year Show, he was gone.

Sally and Thalia said thank you and good-bye to anyone who was listening, mounted their horses, and walked back along the road until they came to a path that led down to the shore. Without a word they turned and rode down over the dunes toward the sea.

"What a day," said Thalia. "And that was some jump."

"Yes, it was," agreed Sally in total satisfaction.

"Do you think he will send us tickets?"

"He might. He said he would."

But it didn't really matter, Sally thought. It

had been good riding Rosie, but only as a special thing. It was Willow that really mattered. Her own horse. Her horse to jump.

"Of course, I'd far rather have Tarquin," said Thalia, reading Sally's thoughts. "Pairs jumping at the Tarent show cross-country? Narg's got the entry forms."

"Okay," said Sally, grinning.

"We'll probably win," laughed Thalia as they let their horses canter on toward the high tower of Kestrel Manor, their heads filled with thoughts of cross-country obstacles as high as the fallen wall with its spread of scattered stones.

"Red ribbons and a cup," Thalia dreamed aloud.

"Red ribbons and a cup," echoed Sally as she put her hand in her pocket and felt the crystal unicorn lying there safe and magic. "I wouldn't be surprised in the least."

Don't miss

Horseshoes

#3

Cross-Country Gallop

Sally and Thalia rode down the hillside to the track, Willow following Tarquin, making high pig squeals of excitement. Thalia let Tarquin gallop on until they reached a stone wall that ran between the trail and the water. It was about two feet high. The land between the wall and the water was short, rough grass.

"You can jump it anywhere," cried Thalia as she swung Tarquin off the track to the right and turned him to jump the wall.

But Sally didn't follow her. There was something not right about the ground on the other side. Somehow the grass looked too smooth, too bright.

Tarquin plunged at the wall. Sally saw him soar out and land. Only he didn't land. He sank through the ground, his legs vanishing instantly, his belly, chest, and quarters sinking more slowly out of sight.

Sally's cries mingled with Tarquin's high, terrible screaming.

In a split second Thalia had torn off her jacket, thrown it across the grass toward the wall, and—squirming her legs free from the bog—launched herself onto it. With a convulsive struggle she reached the firm ground by the wall. Her left hand was clenched on the buckle of Tarquin's reins.

"Get help! Get help!" she cried.